Collect all six Arctica Mermaid books

Also look out for the six original Mermaid SOS adventures in Coral Kingdom

Becky
and the
Stardust
Locket

gillian shields
illustrated by helen Turner

BLOOMSBURY
CHILDREN'S
BOOKS

Underwater
Volcano

Fire Isles

Whaling

Beachcomber
Islands

The Big Waves

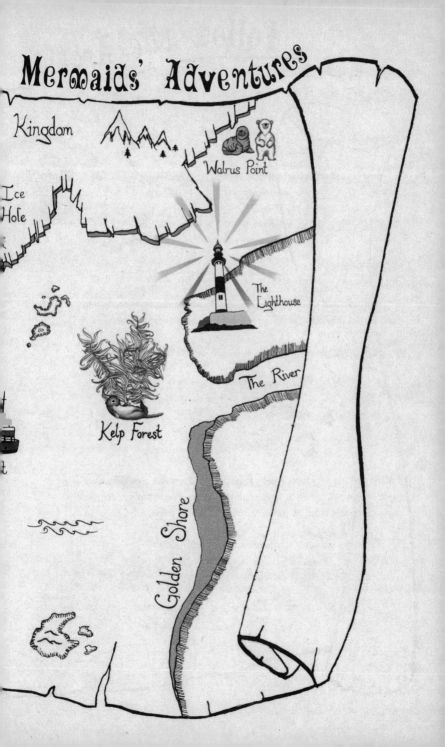

First published in Great Britain in 2007 by Bloomsbury Publishing Plc,
36 Soho Square, London, W1D 3QY

A CIP catalogue record of this book is available from the British Library

ISBN 978 07475 8972 3

Printed and bound in Great Britain by Clays Ltd, St Ives Plc

1 3 5 7 9 10 8 6 4 2

All papers used by Bloomsbury Publishing are natural, recyclable products
made from wood grown in well-managed forests. The manufacturing processes
conform to the environmental regulations of the country of origin.

www.bloomsbury.com/mermaidSOS

For Polly and Sienna
— G.S.

To Bridget,
my super supportive friend!
— Love H.T.

Prologue

When the evil mermaid, Mantora, tried
to destroy Coral Kingdom, she was
outwitted by Misty and her young
mermaid friends. Now she is hatching
another terrible plot! This time it is
against Ice Kingdom, the frozen realm
of Princess Arctica.

Mantora has stolen six precious Snow
Diamonds from the underwater Ice
Cavern. Not only that, she has trapped
Princess Arctica and her good Merfolk

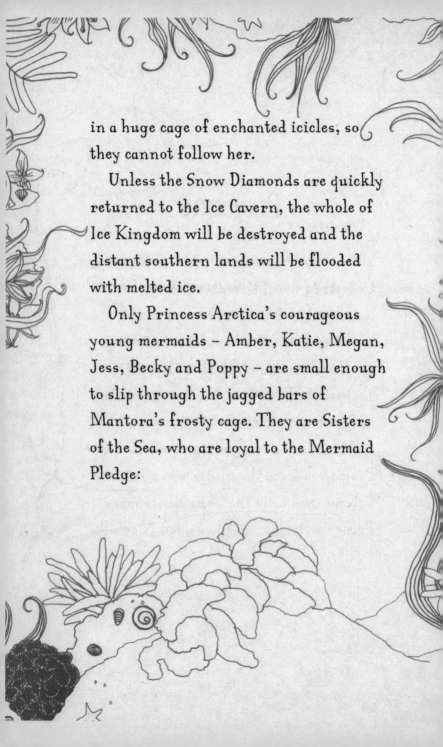

in a huge cage of enchanted icicles, so they cannot follow her.

Unless the Snow Diamonds are quickly returned to the Ice Cavern, the whole of Ice Kingdom will be destroyed and the distant southern lands will be flooded with melted ice.

Only Princess Arctica's courageous young mermaids – Amber, Katie, Megan, Jess, Becky and Poppy – are small enough to slip through the jagged bars of Mantora's frosty cage. They are Sisters of the Sea, who are loyal to the Mermaid Pledge:

We promise that we'll take good care
Of all sea creatures everywhere.
We'll never hurt and never break,
We'll always give and never take.
And as we fight Mantora's threat,
This saying we must not forget:
'I'll help you and you'll help me,
For we are Sisters of the Sea!'

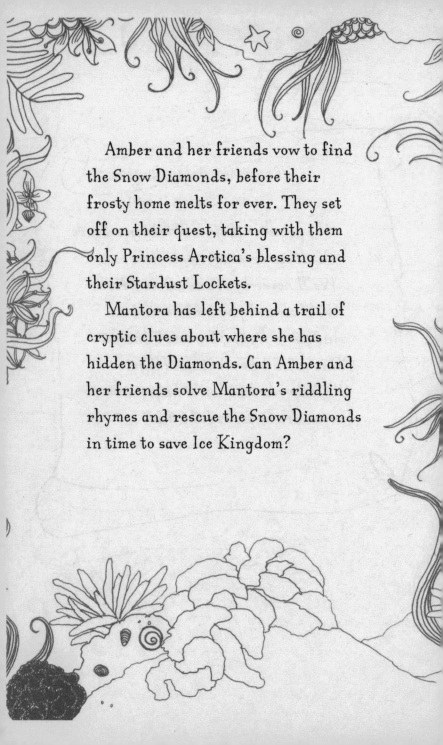

Amber and her friends vow to find the Snow Diamonds, before their frosty home melts for ever. They set off on their quest, taking with them only Princess Arctica's blessing and their Stardust Lockets.

Mantora has left behind a trail of cryptic clues about where she has hidden the Diamonds. Can Amber and her friends solve Mantora's riddling rhymes and rescue the Snow Diamonds in time to save Ice Kingdom?

If you cannot find the Diamonds,
The ice will start to melt.
On all sides of the Ocean,
The danger will be felt.
No more will seals and polar bears
Enjoy their snowy home,
The seas will rise, the lands will flood –
Storm Kingdom will have come!
So try to solve the riddling clues
Of Mantora's cruel game,
But if you fail to work them out,
The world won't be the same ...

Becky

Chapter One

The sun shone on the sparkling blue sea around the Beachcomber Islands. Dolphins were leaping over the waves, and sea birds swooped overhead. But Becky and her mermaid friends – Amber, Katie, Megan, Jess and Poppy – had no time to admire the peaceful scene.

They had travelled from their home in Ice Kingdom with Monty the whale, searching for the Snow Diamonds that had been stolen by Mantora. Now four glittering Diamonds were safe in the Stardust Lockets belonging to Jess, Megan, Katie and Amber. But the flower-shaped Locket that hung from Becky's silver bracelet was still empty.

'I must find a Snow Diamond before it's too late,' Becky thought to herself, swirling

her peach-coloured tail in the waves.
'Thank goodness we've got the fifth clue!'

Becky was clutching a scrap of yellow parchment, scribbled over with Mantora's spidery black handwriting.

'What does it say?' asked the others. 'What have we got to do next?'

Becky began to read Mantora's message:

'Walk, run,

Sing, cheer -

She is very near.

Two legs,

No tail -

Where the boats sail.

Important, precious,

Like a queen -

With her jewels of green.'

19

'It seems like a simple rhyme,' said Amber, 'but it's quite puzzling. Who is this mysterious "*She*" in the clue?'

'Perhaps that's Queen Neptuna,' suggested Katie. 'The clue says it's someone important – like a queen.'

'It's more likely to be Mantora,' replied Megan, protectively cuddling her pet Fairy Shrimp, Sammy. 'She thinks she's the most important person in the whole Ocean. And she's probably got hundreds of green jewels.'

'I hope we won't come face to face with Mantora again,' groaned Becky. 'She's scary! And I'm sure she's still lurking nearby.'

The young mermaids glanced around uneasily. They certainly didn't want to be caught by Mantora.

'Well, I'm not scared of her,' boasted
Poppy. 'Or her mean old Storm Gulls.'

'Poppy, don't be silly,' said Jess, flicking
her strong turquoise tail impatiently. 'You
should be frightened of Mantora. She's very
dangerous.' She lowered her voice to a
whisper. 'And from now on, we must keep
it a secret if we find another Diamond. We
know Mantora wants to snatch them back.
She might be spying on us right now.'

'Good thinking, Jess,' said the others, though Poppy looked rather sulky. She sometimes forgot it was important to work as a team.

'I'm not going to skulk about and whisper, just because Mantora might be nearby,' she declared, her freckled nose stuck in the air. 'If I've got something to say, I'll say it – loud and clear!'

Becky looked up worriedly. The friends couldn't afford to quarrel just now, when there were still two more precious Diamonds to find.

'Calm down, Poppy,' she pleaded. 'Jess is right – we need to stay out of trouble. And look, there's another message from Mantora, scribbled at the bottom of the clue.' She read it aloud:

'You are so near, and yet so far...
This clue is easy, yet so hard...
Don't imagine, my simple-hearted Sisters, that Queen
Neptuna will rush to your aid. She's far too busy to bother
about six insignificant shrimps like you!'

'Shrimps aren't insiggifant...insiffigant
...whatever she said,'
squeaked Sammy
indignantly.
'We know, Sammy,'
smiled Megan, 'you're
very important. And so
is this clue! The
Diamond must be
nearby, but it's still "*far*"
because we haven't worked out what the
riddle means yet.'

24

The mermaids pored over the parchment again, searching for any hints and ideas.

'Why does it tell us to "*walk*" and "*run*" and "*sing*" and "*cheer*"?' asked Jess with a frown. 'Mermaids can't walk and run.'

Becky studied the clue again. Then she looked up and exclaimed, 'No, but someone with "*two legs and no tail*" could.'

'Oh!' chorused the others. 'You mean someone…'

'…Human!' said Becky. 'So the "*She*" in the clue must be a Human woman. And I know where the Humans are.'

She pointed across the foamy waves to the biggest of the Beachcomber Islands. In the distance, the mermaids saw a busy harbour, crowded with boats. Bright sails,

coloured red and green and yellow,
fluttered against the blue sky. Children
played on the sandy beaches on either side
of the harbour.

'Humans!' sighed Megan. 'I'd rather
face an army of Mantora's Storm Gulls
than a single Human. I sometimes think
they're the scariest creatures of all.'

'But our Human friend Ana, the little Inuit girl, cares for the sea and its creatures just as much as we do,' Amber reminded her, as they floated in the warm waves.

'And if the clue tells us to look for a Human woman,' added Becky, 'then that's what we must do.'

'She won't just be an ordinary woman,' Jess pointed out. 'The clue says that she's important. Perhaps she's the chief of the Islands?'

27

'And don't forget the part about "*where the boats sail…*"' added Katie. 'I think we should look near those boats in the harbour.'

Megan gulped, and so did Sammy. 'But it's very dangerous to go near the fishing boats,' she said, her pink and white tail quivering nervously. 'We could easily be caught in their nets.'

'We have no choice,' declared Becky, forcing herself to be brave. 'If we don't solve this clue soon, Ice Kingdom will be lost forever. We'll just have to take the risk. Wish us luck, Monty.'

The huge humpback whale sank down towards the sea bed. 'I'll wait for you young things here,' he said. 'Try to stay out of trouble.'

'We will,' replied the mermaids. 'And we'll come back as soon as we can — hopefully with the fifth Diamond!'

They got ready to swim towards the busy harbour, trying to keep out of sight below the waves. But just as the friends were about to set off, a voice called out:

'Mermaids, ahoy! Stop! S-T-O-P!'

Chapter Two

Becky and the other mermaids twisted round to see who was calling. They saw a smooth grey face, with gleaming eyes and delicate whiskers. It was a monk seal, surging towards them.

'Wait! I'm Luka – wait for me,' he panted. Soon, the plump seal hovered next to the mermaids in the warm waves. 'Did I hear you say you were looking for

Humans? You mustn't go near them. It's too dangerous for young Sisters of the Sea like you!'

'But we must,' said Becky. 'We have to find an important Human woman, who can help us to solve a difficult clue.' She quickly explained about the Snow Diamonds and their quest. Luka's mouth fell open.

31

'I didn't think six little mermaids would be on such an important mission,' he said admiringly. 'There must be more to you than I thought. But I still wouldn't get mixed up with Humans,' he continued, rolling on to his back in the water. 'Oh, they're not all bad, but they seem to be trying to spoil our Islands, with their noise and boats and pleasure trips. Yes, the Islands are changing fast.'

'How do you mean?' asked the mermaids.

'For one thing, haven't you noticed how hot it is? I feel like a toasted jellyfish!' Luka flopped comically on to his front again, trying to keep cool by splashing in the water.

'We do feel warm,' agreed Amber. 'We

are used to the freezing seas of Ice
Kingdom. But isn't it always warm in
your sunny Islands?'

'Not as warm as this,' puffed Luka. 'And
the water levels are rising, too. Some of the
little rocks and islets near here are being
covered up by the sea. I call it downright
unnatural!'

The mermaids glanced at one another
anxiously. Perhaps Ice Kingdom had
already begun to melt, and the whole
world was in danger, just as Mantora had
threatened?

'Thank you for the advice, but our task
is urgent,' said Becky. 'We simply have to
go near the Humans, to look for another
Snow Diamond.'

'And when we have found all six of

them, the world will be safe again,' added Megan softly, 'including your Islands.'

'If it will really help our Island home, I'll help you to find this mysterious Human,' declared Luka, shaking the glittering drops of water from his whiskers. 'Let's call her the Mystery Lady – that will make me feel like a proper detective!'

He thought hard for a moment, then exclaimed, 'There's one woman who is very important in these Islands. And she has a boat called SHINING STAR. That's a bit like a Diamond. Perhaps she is your Mystery Lady?'

'It sounds perfect, Luka,' agreed the mermaids. 'Who is she?'

'We call her the Professor,' said Luka, gazing at them with his lively brown eyes. 'She goes out in her boat every day to watch the dolphins, and make notes about them in her big book. The creatures round here say she is a friend of the sea.'

'Perhaps she's a sort of guardian,' said Becky thoughtfully. 'Princess Arctica told me that some Humans try to look after Mother Nature's world. Let's hope that she can help us.'

'Then come on, everyone,' cried Jess. 'Let's all hunt for the Mystery Lady. *Mermaid SOS!*'

The mermaids slipped through the waves after Luka. He swam away from the busy harbour towards a distant headland. As they rounded the headland, the young friends saw a lonely cove, with palm trees growing from the dunes on the beach. A small red boat was anchored in the bay. The letters SHINING STAR were painted in white on its side.

'That must be the Professor's boat,' murmured Katie, as they hid by the headland. 'She's watching those spinner dolphins.'

Becky saw a kind-faced Human lady, with glasses and brown hair. She was jotting things down in her scientific notebook, and smiling as she watched the dolphins leaping through the waves.

'I think the Professor does love the sea and its creatures,' Becky said, in a low voice. 'But is she really the Human that we're looking for?'

'And how can we search the SHINING STAR for the Diamond, without her noticing us?' added Jess.

Luka turned to the mermaids, his smooth grey face wrinkling with laughter.

'Watch me,' he grinned. 'I've got an idea!'

He quickly swam over to where the boat bobbed up and down. Then the plucky seal started to twist and turn in the water, making a strange barking noise. It was a peculiar sight – and sound! Even the dolphins were surprised, and hastily swam away.

The Professor watched the seal's antics intently, leaning over the side of her boat and scribbling in her notebook. Then Luka looked over his shoulder at the mermaids, nodding his head and winking.

'He's telling us to search the boat whilst the Professor has her back turned,' whispered Becky. 'Jess – and you too, Poppy – you're fast and strong. Could you please do it?'

'But won't she see us?' asked Jess.

'Not if you swim under the water to the far side of the SHINING STAR,' replied Becky. 'Follow me!'

Soon, Jess and Poppy were wriggling silently over the edge of the little red boat, helped by the others. Very quickly and quietly, the brave young friends searched through the bags and boxes which lay in the bottom of the boat. As they did so, the

comical seal twisted and danced in the blue sea. The Professor had never seen anything like it, and she didn't take her eyes off him for a second.

But Jess and Poppy soon sank quietly back into the waves.

'It's no good,' they said, as all the mermaids plunged underwater again. 'The Diamond's not there. The only "*shining star*" is in the boat's name.'

'That's so disappointing,' sighed Becky. 'Luka seemed sure that the Professor would be the Mystery Lady.'

'Sorry – I must have been wrong!' said a cheerful voice. It was Luka, twisting and turning through the group of mermaids. 'But I can take you to another important woman. She wears something shiny round her neck. That might be the Diamond you are looking for.'

'It might – or it might not!' said Poppy impatiently. 'This is all too vague for me.'

Becky and the mermaids looked at one another other doubtfully, not sure what to do. Then a little voice piped up.

'If at first you don't succeed, try and try

again,' said the tiny Fairy Shrimp, puffing his chest out bravely.

'You're right, Sammy,' smiled Becky. 'And I think this is definitely worth a try. Lead the way, Luka!'

The mermaids swam after the seal with a ripple of their glistening tails. As they all sped away under the water, the Professor watched Luka through her binoculars.

'I've never seen a seal behave like that,' she murmured. 'And now he's swimming with a whole group of his folk. But I've never seen seals with pink and purple tails!' The curious scientist lowered her binoculars and blinked in surprise. 'Oh dear, I must have got a touch of the sun.' Then she laughed, and added, 'Or perhaps it's a touch of magic…'

Chapter Three

Becky and the mermaids raced towards a
wide bay, where rolling waves crashed on
the shore.

'Why are we going here?' she asked Luka.

'Because that's where we'll find the
Champ!' replied Luka.

'Who's that?' wondered Amber, as she
swam just behind Becky and the friendly
seal.

'The Champion surfer – the Human I was telling you about,' said Luka. 'She's called Lana. And here comes the surf, so watch out!'

'Ooooohh!' squealed the mermaids. A huge wave pulled them up to the top of its crest, then tipped them over into the splashing surf.

Becky shook the sea spray from her eyes and looked up. For a split second she caught sight of a young woman in a wet suit, skimming the glassy surface of the sea on a surfboard. It was Lana! Perhaps she was the Mystery Lady? And was the shiny thing round her neck the Snow Diamond? But before Becky had time to see any more, another huge wave sucked her under the water.

'Catch hold of my hand!' shouted Katie. The mermaids were all clinging on to one another under the swelling sea.

'Becky! Stay with us!' yelled Jess. 'We don't want to get lost in this surf.'

But Becky shook her head, with a determined expression on her face. She *had* to find out whether it really was the Diamond that she'd just glimpsed. The brave little mermaid fought her way back up to the surface, gasping in the mass of foaming water. Then Becky paddled through the waves on her tummy, as if she was lying on a surfboard. She tried to keep her glistening tail out of sight. Soon, the water heaved into a high, rolling wave.

Over the crest came Lana again. She was crouched over her board, her arms balanced and her eyes focussed. Something flashed gold on a chain round her neck. Out of the corner of her eye, she noticed Becky floating in the swell. Lana looked surprised, and lost her balance. She fell off her board with an astonished gasp, then swam swiftly to the shore.

'How strange!' Lana said to herself. 'I'm sure I saw a…but I couldn't have! They don't exist…do they?' She shook her head in disbelief. 'Perhaps I've done enough for one day. It's time to go home.'

Lana picked her surfboard out of the shallows. She stared at the rolling sea, searching for the flash of a glittering tail. But Becky was already deep under the crashing surf once more, glad to be with her friends again.

'It's not a Diamond round her neck,' she puffed. 'It's a little gold necklace shaped like a dolphin, which sparkled in the sun.'

'Oh dear,' said Amber, with a sigh. 'Time is running out, and we're no nearer to finding our Mystery Lady – or the fifth Diamond! Whatever are we going to do?'

'I'm sorry Lana wasn't right, but I've thought of someone else you should investigate,' said Luka brightly. 'It will be one last try.'

The mermaids looked unsure, though Becky was determined not to give up.

'We can't stop now,' she pleaded with

her friends. 'This might be third time lucky. I think we should trust Luka.'

'Come on, mermaids,' cried the cheerful seal. 'Follow me back to the harbour!'

As the mermaids sped after him under the waves, it was beginning to get dark in the Overwater world. The sun glowed crimson, and the Evening Star shone pure and high above the Beachcomber Islands.

Becky looked up through the clear water at the milk-white star. It reminded her of the great North Star, shining far away over her icy home. A beam of

49

its silvery light had been magically wrought into her Stardust Locket, like a sprinkling of frost. But Becky's Locket was still empty.

'*Starlight, Star Bright, show us what we seek tonight…*' she whispered. 'I must find the fifth Diamond soon!'

Her thoughts were interrupted by Luka. 'We're near the harbour now,' he said in a low voice. 'Don't let anyone see you.'

The friends swam silently underneath the waves, weaving in and out of the small boats that were anchored for the night. Luka was heading for a beach near the edge of the harbour. As the mermaids followed him up to the surface, Becky found that they were hidden by a low mound of rocks that separated the waves from the shore.

On the other side of the rocks, a simple
wooden building stood on the beach.

The building was decorated with strings
of coloured lights. People were sitting at
little round tables, enjoying their supper in
the warm evening air. Children played on
the sand, digging
holes and
looking for
shells.

Becky and her friends kept well out of sight behind the rocks.

'Where are we, Luka?' whispered Becky.

The seal waved his flipper at a large sign that was nailed over the doorway of the wooden house. It said:

THE DI'MOND DINER –
BEST FOOD ON THE ISLAND!

'This is Mama Kala's Diner,' he replied. 'Now, she's a *very* important woman. She runs this café, as well as looking after her family. I really do think she might be the Mystery Lady – and just look at her sparkly earrings! Don't you think they could be made of diamonds?'

At that moment, Mama Kala came out.

The simple wooden house was her home, as well as the kitchen for her café. She was carrying a huge tray of tasty-looking food, which she set down in front of her customers with a smile. Mama Kala was no longer young, but she had a jolly round face, flowers in her hair, and glittery earrings. But the mermaids' sharp eyes saw that they were made from shells and beads, not from a precious Snow Diamond.

'Oh, this is hopeless,' muttered Poppy in disgust. As usual she was speaking before she was thinking, and her words sounded rather rude. 'Luka hasn't shown us anyone who really is this stupid Mystery Lady. We're just wasting our time. Let's go and find some other creatures who can help us properly.'

A hurt expression flashed over the seal's friendly grey face. The other mermaids felt sorry for him. They knew that Luka was trying his best.

'Poppy!' said Megan quietly.

'That's not a very nice thing to say.
We should be grateful to Luka.'

'Oh, I am,' gabbled Poppy impatiently.
'I just want to get on with finding the
Diamond. Becky and I still haven't filled
our Stardust Lockets. Becky – what do you
think we should do? Becky?'

But Becky didn't answer. The dreamy
young mermaid was peeping over the rocks
and staring intently at the children on the
beach.

'Becky?' called Katie softly. 'What do
you think?'

'I think we've found what we are
searching for,' said Becky, her voice
trembling with excitement. 'Look!'

Chapter Four

Becky was pointing at a group of young children. They were playing in the last light of the sunset, whilst their parents finished their meal at the Diner. The carefree youngsters were running races and cheering the winners, or clapping their hands and singing, or sailing toy boats in the warm shallows.

'Don't you see?' asked Becky eagerly, as

her friends gathered round her. 'They're doing all the things mentioned in the clue! Walking, running, singing, cheering — they are even playing with boats. It's not an important "Mystery Lady" that we need to find — it's a little child!'

'Of course,' breathed Megan. 'What could be more important than one of these children? You're so clever, Becky.'

'Well done, Becky,' said Katie. 'You've worked it all out.'

'I couldn't have done it without Luka helping us,' said Becky. She swished her glinting tail and turned to the seal. 'I'm so glad you brought us here.'

'I knew it would be third time lucky,' Luka grinned. He poked Poppy slyly in the ribs with his flipper. 'How about that then, Miss Impatient?'

'All right, all right,' said Poppy, with her nose in the air. 'I admit we seem to have come to the right place at last. But look at all those children! How can we tell which is the one we want?

Becky's face fell. Poppy was right; they hadn't solved the whole clue yet.

'It must be a girl,' she replied slowly, 'because the clue said "*like a queen*". And

it said that she had green jewels. But none
of these girls are wearing jewels.'

Like Mama Kala, the little girls wore
pretty necklaces and earrings made of
shells and gleaming pebbles. But there
were no green jewels anywhere. And one by
one, the children and their families were
starting to leave the beach.

'We can't do any more tonight,' said
Amber. 'We're all tired and the children
are going home to bed. Let's rest, hidden
by these rocks, and see what the new day
brings. I'm sure the children will come
back to the beach tomorrow.'

'Oh, but we can't stop now…' began
Becky.

'We'll have to,' said Jess firmly. 'A rest
will do us good. Come on, we can all

snuggle down together. Thank you so much for your help, Luka.'

Luka danced in the water for one last time, waggling his flippers to make the mermaids smile.

'Just call if you need me again, Sisters of the Sea,' he cried.

'Thank you,' the mermaids replied softly. 'You were an excellent detective! Goodbye!'

Very soon, the lights of the Di'mond Diner were put out, and Mama Kala shut the wooden door.

Everyone had gone home. Becky lay hidden on a smooth shelf of rock. She looked up at the faraway stars, remembering what Princess Arctica had said about the Stardust Lockets' magical powers. 'Show me what to do next,' she murmured, gently touching her Locket. 'Show me...what...to...do...' Soon she was fast asleep.

As Becky slept, she had a deep dream – a vision of a beautiful mermaid. A glimmering Crystal was bound across her brows like a crown. The queenly mermaid brushed her shining hair and pinned it up with a jewelled comb. Her sweet voice echoed through Becky's slumbers:

'*Look for the child with the Mermaid Comb, my Sister. Look for the Mermaid Comb...*'

When Becky woke up, the new day was
dawning. Everything was still and clear.
There was no one on the beach yet. Becky
quickly woke the others, shaking them
gently.

'I've seen her!' she said excitedly.

'Who have you seen? What do you
mean?' yawned Katie, as she tried to wake
up properly.

'Have you seen the little girl we need to

find?' added Amber, blinking in the early morning light.

'No!' replied Becky. 'I've seen Queen Neptuna, and she spoke to me!' She started to explain about her strange dream. 'It was the Mermaid Magic telling me what to do, I'm sure of it. We have to find a girl with a Mermaid Comb in her hair!'

But just then, Becky was interrupted by the sound of singing. It was coming from Mama Kala's Diner. One voice was low and husky, and the other was sweet and high, like a skylark: '*Good morning to the bright new day, another chance to work and play...*'

Becky and her friends peered across the waves from the shelter of their rocks. The

mermaids saw Mama Kala flinging open the Diner's wooden doors as she sang, followed by a little girl they hadn't seen before.

'I'll tidy up out here, Granny,' said the girl, giving Mama Kala a kiss. 'You sit down and rest.'

'Sit and rest!' repeated Mama Kala, her plump body quivering with laughter. 'I can't be resting, you precious child. I've got too much to do. But I'll go in, Maya, and make you the best breakfast you ever tasted.'

Maya smiled and started to sweep the crumbs from the tables and chairs, where the customers had sat the night before. She sang happily as she worked, but her hair kept falling into her eyes, so she took a comb from her pocket. Twisting her hair into a thick strand, Maya pinned it back with the carved comb, then turned round to carry on with her chores. As she did so, the mermaids saw that the hair fastener was set with gleaming stones, the colour of spring leaves.

'Green jewels,' gasped Megan. 'She's wearing a Mermaid Comb in her hair.'

'So she's the child Queen Neptuna told

me to look for,' said Becky eagerly. 'The Magic has shown her to us at last!'

Even Poppy looked impressed. 'How can we ask her if she's seen the Diamond?' she asked.

'I don't think we need to ask her that,' said Amber faintly. 'Just look at her…'

The girl had finished tidying and was sitting on one of the wooden chairs. She looked round to make sure that her Granny, Mama Kala, wasn't watching. Then she took something from her pocket – a shining object which gleamed and glittered with a hundred magical colours.

It was the fifth Snow Diamond!

Chapter Five

Maya held the Diamond up to catch the sun's rays.

'You're so pretty,' she said. 'Granny will be happy when she sees her birthday present.' Then she put the jewel safely in her pocket again.

The mermaids looked at one another in dismay.

'Do you think the girl has...*stolen*...the

Diamond from Mantora?' whispered
Poppy, in a shocked voice.

'No,' replied Becky. 'My heart tells me
to trust this girl. We must speak to her
and get to the bottom of the mystery.
Gosh, we really are turning into detectives,
just like Luka said.' She paused and then
added, 'We'll need your music now, Katie.'

Katie was always ready to play and sing
for her friends. Quickly lifting her
Mermaid Harp from her shoulder, she
softly strummed the strings and sang:

> *'Little girl, your friends are near,*
> *This song is just for you to hear.'*

Standing up in surprise, Maya walked
down to the edge of the shore, trying to

find out where the music had come from.

Becky sang sweetly:

'I am a Sister of the Sea –
Will you come and speak to me?'

As she sang, Becky looked out from behind the rocks, so that she could be seen as well as heard. Maya jumped nervously when she noticed her.

'Is it you again?' she cried, looking strangely worried. She splashed through the shallow waves with her bare legs and scrambled on to the rocks. 'But you're not the same as before,' she said, staring round at the mermaids in relief. 'And there are more of you this time.'

'What do you mean?' said Becky, in a friendly voice.

'It's not the first time I have seen a mermaid,' replied Maya. 'I couldn't tell anyone, because I promised to keep it a secret. I wanted to last night, though, when I was helping Granny in the kitchen.'

'Why was that, Maya?' Megan asked.

'Because everyone who came to the Diner was chattering about the Merfolk,' replied the little girl. 'Granny says the whole Island has mermaid fever, even the Professor. And people were saying that Lana, the Champion surfer, had seen a

mermaid on a surfboard! But I really *have*
seen one before.'

'Let me guess,' said Jess grimly. 'Was
this mermaid bigger than us, with a long
veil and a glinting crown?'

Maya looked confused, and even a little
bit frightened.

'How did you know?' she asked.

'Listen, Maya,' urged Becky. 'We know
you have something very important.
And I'm sorry to say that it
belongs to the Merfolk.'

'Do you mean my Mermaid Comb?'
asked Maya, taking the trinket from her
hair. 'My cousin, Jack, who lives far across
the ocean, sent it to me.'

She held the comb up, so that its green
gems gleamed like cat's eyes.

'It's so pretty, isn't it?' Maya continued.
'When Jack wrote that a mermaid had
given it to him,
I thought he was
making up a story
for fun. But now
I know that mermaids
really do exist!'
She held it out to
Becky. 'You must
have this back,
if it belongs to you.'

72

Becky took a deep breath. 'It's not the Mermaid Comb that we are looking for, Maya,' she explained. 'We are seeking something much more important than that.'

'We need the Snow Diamond,' interrupted Poppy. 'We must have it to save our home in Ice Kingdom!'

Now Maya's eyes grew even bigger with worry.

'Do you mean my sparkly stone?' she asked. 'But I can't let you have that – I want to give it to Granny for her birthday next week. And besides, the mermaid who gave it to me also gave me a warning.' Maya lowered her voice to a whisper. 'She said that if I gave it to anyone outside my family, a terrible Storm

Curse would fall on the whole Island, and that all the seals and fish and dolphins would die!'

'That sounds like Mantora all right,' muttered Poppy.

'When did you see this other mermaid, Maya?' asked Megan.

'The night before last,' the little girl replied. 'It was hot and I couldn't sleep. I heard someone calling my name outside. I didn't want to disturb Granny, so I slipped out of the door. There was a mermaid sitting on the rocks, near the sands. She had a veil, just like you said. It was a little bit spooky, because I couldn't see her face. She gave me the stone – the Diamond – and she made me promise not to tell anyone. Who was she?'

The mermaids gathered closer round Maya.

'That was Mantora,' said Amber solemnly. 'She is a great enemy to all true Merfolk, and to you Humans, too. She doesn't care about the seals or dolphins, or about the children of the world. And we need the Snow Diamonds to defeat her wicked plans.'

'Well...' hesitated Maya. 'I like you much better than I liked her. She was bossy, and she scared me with her talk of the Storm Curse. But I'm

frightened to give you the Diamond, because you're not my family. I love the sea creatures – I don't want to curse the whole Island!'

Just then, Mama Kala's husky warm voice called out from the wooden house. 'Maya! Breakfast is ready…'

Maya looked round quickly. 'I've got to go,' she said. 'Granny doesn't believe in the Merfolk. She says Lana must have had sunstroke, "babbling crazy tales" like that.'

'Wait,' said Becky, 'we need to talk to you about…'

'M-a-y-a!'

'I can't stay,' said Maya, scrambling down from the rocks. 'But I promise I'll see you tonight. Come to the little bay where the Professor keeps her boat. Meet me there at moonrise.'

She splashed back to the beach, running home for her breakfast. There was nothing the mermaids could do now but wait. Would Maya keep her promise? And would she bring the Snow Diamond to their moonlight meeting?

Chapter Six

The mermaids had spent the day out at
sea with Monty, hiding from the passing
fishing boats. Now, at last, the moon was
rising over the Islands like a silver penny.
It was time to look for Maya.

Becky and her friends swam under the
stars to the lonely cove, where the
Professor's red boat had been dragged on
to the sand.

'I don't think Maya has come,' said Becky, in a disappointed voice.

Just then, however, Maya's silky head peeped over the side of the boat. The little girl waved, as the mermaids glided to the edge of the shore and sat on their sparkling tails. Then Maya took the Snow Diamond from her pocket. It gleamed like a star on the palm of her hand.

'I do want to help save Ice Kingdom,'
she said quietly. 'It's just that I'm so
worried about Mantora's Storm Curse. I
don't want anything bad to happen
because of me. But if I don't give you the
Diamond, Ice Kingdom will be destroyed!
Oh, what shall I do?'

Maya shook her head in confusion and
burst into tears.

'Mantora just made up that mean curse
story to scare you,' Megan said, squeezing
the little girl's hand gently.

'Scary old Mantora,' squeaked Sammy.
'She's very bad!'

'Yes, she only told you to keep the
Diamond in your family so that we would
never find it,' said Amber.

'Are you sure?' sniffed Maya, glancing

round at the eager young mermaids.

'I'm sure,' said Becky kindly. 'And besides, anyone who takes the Mermaid Pledge becomes our true Sister.'

Maya looked interested and seemed to brighten up a little.

'The Mermaid Pledge?' she asked. 'What's that?'

'Come into the water and we'll show you!' smiled Becky.

Jumping up from the sand, Maya paddled a little way into the warm sea. The mermaids slipped into the waves, and swam around her in a graceful Mermaid Dance.

'Repeat this after us,' they called gaily, and then began to sing:

'We promise that we'll take good care
Of all sea creatures everywhere.
We'll never hurt and never break,
We'll always give and never take.
And as we fight Mantora's threat,
This saying we must not forget:
"I'll help you and you'll help me,
For we are Sisters of the Sea!"'

'There,' said Becky, giving Maya a hug when the singing was over. 'Now we really are sisters – all one family.'

'In that case, here is the Diamond that belongs to the Merfolk,' said Maya happily, as they settled by the edge of the waves again. She pressed the precious jewel into Becky's hand. Becky was so thankful to have the fifth Diamond safe at last!

'Thank you so much, Maya,' she said, gratefully hiding the wonderful Diamond in her Stardust Locket.

'Your Locket is so beautiful,' sighed Maya. 'I wish I had something pretty to give Granny for her birthday, now that I don't have the Diamond any more.'

'Perhaps there is something in Ana's bag

that Maya would like to take for Mama
Kala?' suggested Amber.

She pulled open the soft pouch which
hung by her side. It contained some plaited
ropes, a silk handkerchief, some bright
Inuit beads and carvings, as well as other
bits and pieces. But there was nothing
quite as splendid as the Snow Diamond.

Becky glanced down at her Stardust Locket which hung from her silver bracelet, like a flower of sparkling ice. She was so proud of it and felt as though she couldn't bear to part with it.

'Maya, you gave me the Snow Diamond, which is the most important gift of all,' Becky stammered. She took a deep breath. 'So you can have my Stardust Locket to give to Mama Kala. I can keep the Diamond tied up in that handkerchief that belonged to Ana.' The other mermaids looked on, open-mouthed. Becky was being so generous!

'No, no, it's too much, I really can't take it...' protested Maya.

But at that moment, they all fell silent. Bright rays of silver light suddenly

poured from Becky's Stardust Locket and
danced in front of their eyes. Coloured
sparkles streamed out from all the other
Lockets, until a glittering fountain of light
and colour shot into the air like a rainbow.

'It's Mermaid Magic,' gasped Becky.

The rainbow of light streamed down on
to Becky's hand, then there was a blinding
flash. When she opened her fingers, a
shining object lay there. It was an exact
twin of Becky's Stardust Locket, just as
beautiful as the original.

'So now there is one Locket for Becky

and one for Maya!' said the stunned mermaids. 'And you both deserve them.'

'I shall give mine to Granny for her birthday,' exclaimed Maya, as she picked it up carefully. 'I'll never forget that you offered to give me yours, Becky! I think the Magic must have heard you being so kind and unselfish.'

'And this is for you, Maya,' said a tiny voice.

Whilst the others had been watching the enchanted Stardust Locket come to life, Sammy had struggled to thread some of

Ana's bright Inuit beads on to a leather
string. The little shrimp blushed bright red
as he gave the dainty necklace to Maya.
'You must have something pretty, too.'

'Oh, that's so lovely,' said Maya. 'Here,
why don't you take the Mermaid Comb
back to Ice Kingdom, Sammy? Please give
it to Ana, to say thank you for these lovely

beads. I'm sure Jack would like me to do that.'

'So many presents!' chirped Sammy, as they exchanged gifts.

'Giving and sharing are very important to the Sisters of the Sea,' said Becky seriously. 'And Maya really is one of us now.'

The mermaids gave the little girl one final hug, then watched her race away home over the sand. They could imagine the astonishment on Mama Kala's face when she saw the new Stardust Locket. Maya's Granny would have to believe in the Merfolk after this!

'I suppose we must get back to work,' said Jess practically, as the mermaids started to swim away from the beach.

'Was there a clue with the Diamond, Becky? We must find out what to do next.'

'I know what I'm going to do next,' boasted Poppy loudly, turning a splashy somersault in the waves. 'I'm going to find the sixth Snow Diamond! Nothing can stop us now that we've found the other five.'

'Shhh!' said Katie and Amber warningly. 'Remember, some of Mantora's spies might be lurking around.' But Poppy was too excited to listen.

'I don't care if she knows. Now that we've found five, we'll easily find the last one,' Poppy exclaimed, twirling her silver bracelet happily. 'And the sixth Diamond will be for my very own Stardust Locket.'

'Oh, will it?' said a sneering, hissing voice. 'I wouldn't be so sure of that, my beauty.'

The mermaids whipped round in the water, struck with horror, as they recognised the terrifying voice. A cloud passed over the moon and seemed to blot out all the stars. Storm Gulls swept over the horizon. The waves began to swell until they were dark and menacing. A cloaked shape arose from the suddenly choppy sea. It was Mantora! She had overheard Poppy's boastful chatter, and now she had the little mermaids in her power at last.

Mantora thrust her netted spear aloft
and chanted a powerful spell:

> '**Sleep so deep –**
> **And when you wake,**
> **You will weep.**'

A dark mist swirled over the mermaids,
making them feel confused and sleepy.
Becky tried to fight it, and struggled to
keep her eyes open. But the words of the
evil charm whirled through her head like a
storm…*sleep…deep…sleep…deep…*She
felt as though she was falling into a deep,
dark prison…

Soon, all the little mermaids lay helpless
in an enchanted sleep on the edge of the
shore. Mantora muttered another spell,

and the five sparkling Snow Diamonds flew from the Stardust Lockets straight into her greedy hands.

'Ha, ha, ha!' she shrieked. 'Lie there, my mermaids, and awake to a bitter surprise!' She threw a black parchment on to the sand, and plunged under the heaving waves. Then Mantora darted away, followed by her Storm Gulls, leaving only silence behind her.

Was this the end of the mermaids' quest? And would the Sisters of the Sea be too late to save Ice Kingdom, when they woke from their enchanted sleep?

Amber has golden curls and a gleaming lilac tail. She looks after her friends, and is a good leader.

Katie enjoys playing her Mermaid Harp. She has a long plait over her shoulder and a sparkly lemon-coloured tail.

Megan has sweet wavy hair and a spangled pink and white tail. She is never far from her pet Fairy Shrimp, Sammy.

Jess is bold and brave, with dark curls and a dazzling turquoise tail. She is friends with Monty, the humpback whale.

Becky loves the beauty of the sea. Her hair is decorated with flowers, and her tail is a pretty peach colour.

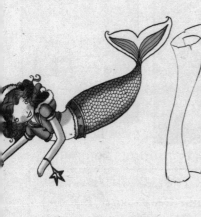

Poppy has coppery curls, a bright blue tail, and bags of confidence, but her impatience can land her in trouble.